The
ADVENTURES
of COURAGE,
THE BIG BAD
STALLION

Courage

HEART AND
DESIRE

T A Fincher

Theresa Fincher

Wasteland Press
www.wastelandpress.net
Shelbyville, KY USA

The Adventures of Courage, The Big Bad Stallion:
Heart and Desire
by Theresa Fincher

Copyright © 2013 Theresa Fincher
ALL RIGHTS RESERVED

Second Printing – September 2013
ISBN: 978-1-60047-871-0
Illustrations by Rachel Dunn

EXCEPT FOR BRIEF TEXT QUOTED AND APPROPRIATELY CITED IN
OTHER WORKS, NO PART OF THIS BOOK MAY BE REPRODUCED IN
ANY FORM, BY PHOTOCOPYING OR BY ELECTRONIC OR
MECHANICAL MEANS, INCLUDING INFORMATION STORAGE
OR RETRIEVAL SYSTEMS, WITHOUT PERMISSION IN WRITING
FROM THE COPYRIGHT OWNER/AUTHOR.

Printed in the U.S.A.

0   1   2   3   4   5   6   7   8   9   10   11   12

ACKNOWLEDGEMENTS

I'd like to thank the following people for their contributions to the Courage book series. First and foremost, I want to thank my horses: Wriggley, Rabano and Blue. They each contribute to the horse's characters in this book, and I would not have material if it wasn't for their colorful personalities!

I'd like to thank my husband, Rhett, he is not only the spirit behind Zander's horseman traits, but he is my daily support system in my writing of this series, affording me the ability to stay focused on my dreams. Rhett also gets a co-author status for helping me with the skeleton of Heart and Desire as well as his help in creative editing of this book.

I'd like to thank Jan Evans for editing and Rachel Dunn for illustrations in both Prey Meets Predator and Heart and Desire. Thank you to all my friends for their support in my efforts toward this series and a special thank you to Pat Parelli for his mentorship, Martin Black for his technical assistance, Bill and Susan Casner for providing me a beautiful facility in TX to write Heart and Desire along with their continued support and encouragement with the series.

Last but not least, thank you, Polly Craig, for believing and marketing my Courage project, helping me get this series to horse crazy kids as well as adults so they can learn more about their horses and see the authentic connection to the spirit of the horse.

Thank you to everyone who has purchased and supported the Courage project.

With Love,
Theresa and Courage

Chapter One

It was a cool invigorating spring morning with a mild breeze and crystal clear blue skies. The morning sunlight glistened on the snow covered mountain peaks creating beauty, stillness and peace.

Courage's herd was grazing just a few short miles away from any civilization, and young handsome Courage was playing heartily and mischievously within his herd.

"I am a Big... I am a Brave..." Courage sang as he cantered away from his herd, bucking playfully. "I am a Fun.... I am a Cool..." he continued to sing as he romped back toward his herd trotting up next to Adri, his older sister. "I am a HANDSOME... STALLION... Oh Yes I am, Oh Yes I am... Uh huh, Uh huh... Oh Yes I am!" he continued to hum as he pranced alongside Adri with a playful grin while eyeing her mischievously.

Adri gave Courage a stern look from the corner of her eye. The energetic stallion was fully aware of the warning, but he just smiled then giggled as he continued to prance alongside her, crowding her space just a bit more. Adri pinned her ears and gave Courage a more intense and stern glare. He noticed this warning as well but persisted in annoying Adri anyway. He resumed prancing alongside the irritated filly and ever so slowly stretched his neck out, curled his lips up and quickly delivered a playful nip to her neck.

The surprised filly leaped away from the playful stallion, she turned and kicked, just barely grazing his hind end. Courage bound into the air with glee "Woo Hoo!" Courage hooted.

"When are you going to learn to stay out of my space?" Adri scolded young Courage as she trotted to the other side of the herd.

"Well, I guess she doesn't want to play with ME!" Courage exclaimed with a chuckle. The young energetic stallion trotted forward sneaking into position just behind Tanner, his older brother. Courage slowly and carefully reached out his neck and swiftly nipped his brother on the hind end.

Tanner jumped straight up then turned and faced Courage. They immediately started rearing and playing. They anchored their hind legs on the ground, which freed up their front legs to box the air toward each other.

"I bet you can't move my feet!" Tanner taunted Courage. Tanner was a year older than Courage and was darker in color and much stouter. Both horses loved to play games with each other.

"I bet I can!" Courage responded playfully. Courage bobbed his head up and down, energetically half rearing. He reached out his neck and leaned over toward Tanner, pinning his ears and baring his front teeth. Tanner dodged away from Courage, but young Courage instantly nipped him on the withers.

"Ouch!" Tanner shrieked as he dove in the opposite direction.

"I moved your feeeet, I moved your feeeet, yes I did, oh YES I did!" Courage sang as he strutted.

"Let's try that again!" Tanner challenged. Courage giggled and started half rearing again, raising his front hooves preparing for their next round. Both horses secured their hind legs to the earth, sparring and nipping each other, playing vivaciously. Courage would move Tanner's feet and then Tanner would move Courage's. Back and forth, back and forth until their mother, Gal, locked her eyes on them and walked slowly and sternly in their direction. Her energy thundered toward them with every step she took. The colts knew it was in their best interest to respect her warning and brought all four feet to the ground in one big hurry.

Courage sheepishly looked up at his mother and saw the stern look in her eye, the one that told him he was one step away from a colossal wallop. The young spirited stallion lowered his head, blew out his nostrils, and gave his whole body a shake. Courage slowly turned around watching his mother out of the corner of his eye and walked softly and cautiously away angling his hindquarters in a position that a whack would hurt much less! Gal rolled her eyes, shook her head and grinned. She slowly turned and walked back to the other side of the herd taking her place next to the colt's father, Roman.

"I see yet once again our feisty young stallion is causing disorder within the herd!" Roman said to Gal with a big grin.

Gal observed Courage from across the herd, admiring him for his curiosity and spirited nature. She knew Courage was destined for something very special.

Courage was very handsome and a tall, leggy colt, with a rich brown color, beautiful soft eyes, and a white star on his forehead. She thought back to when Courage was gone for so long and how afraid she was that she would never see her brave son again, and there he appeared in their time of need. Oh how scared she had been when that bad human tried to take her daughter, Adri. Her heart had cried out for her little filly to be saved. She had been so frightened for her family and for Roman, who was holding the bad humans at bay. Out of nowhere her brave son had emerged with sheer determination and saved her family. Gal sighed, beaming with pride and answered, "Yes, yes he is causing disorder and isn't it just perfect!"

Chapter Two

Courage noticed his mother, Gal, proudly watching him. He knew how frightened she had been when those bad humans tried to steal Adri away from his family.

He then looked over at his father and recalled the day when his dad asked him to step away from the herd soon after his return. "Son, let's take a walk," his father had said to him as he nudged him away from the herd. Courage had been jumpy because he had thought that he was in BIG trouble and he had been afraid his dad would deliver a wallop when he least expected it. Instead his father only had walked in silence next to his young son. It was as if his father had been trying to choose the right words to speak to him.

They had walked for quite awhile, and his father finally broke the silence, "Son, I've listened quietly while you told stories of your adventures with the young human boy named Zander, your horse friends, Mia and Shalot, and about the bad man who took Shalot away from her home and family. I thought you should know that I was aware of your visits to your friend's home and I knew exactly where you were when you did not return. I've always kept my eye on you, young Courage," he divulged as he reached down to take a bite of grass.

"You did?" Courage asked in surprise.

"Son, you don't think you're the only clever stallion in the herd, do you?" Roman winked. "When you were injured, your friend, Mia, would let me know every day how your recovery was coming along," his dad revealed. Courage seemed to be surprised by his father's disclosure, which triggered his father to continue. "She didn't tell you about my visits because I asked her not to, and I think it is time I share some things with you son. When I spoke to you about bad humans, I told you this because I, and …well …your mother know from experience how cruel humans can be to our kind. We know this because… well because… we lived among humans at one time." Roman became still once again.

Courage was puzzled but remained quiet as he processed what his father had told him. Finally he nodded and blew loudly out his nostrils. *His father and mother had lived amongst humans?* "Father, where? When? I want to know all about it!" he pleaded.

"Well, Son, let me just say that there are some humans that naturally understand or learned from their elders that we are ALL connected. It doesn't matter if we are in horse or human form, we are meant to join each other, to not only get work accomplished but to … well, evolve to make us individually and collectively better. The humans that have this understanding learn how to communicate with us and become our partners, treating us with dignity, respect and love." his father paused. "Well, such as your human friend, Zander. This boy reminds me quite a bit of an older human named Jackson that I once knew when I was younger. The boy looks a lot like him and communicates with you in the same way that the older man communicated with me," his father recalled. "But son, there are also humans that haven't yet come to this understanding and view us only as servants to them because they see our kind as objects, they want us to serve their human purpose because they don't understand our shared purpose. Some of these humans that don't understand how to communicate with us can get frustrated and angry because of their lack of understanding and well, Son, it can turn into force, intimidation and downright cruelty. Unfortunately, the humans that don't understand … well… those sort of humans were whom your mother and I were sold to," Roman declared as he looked back and observed his herd.

The young stallion's eyes widened then he blinked several times and widened his eyes once again. "Wow!!" Courage exclaimed. "Wow, Wow, WOW, Father!" he repeated in amazement.

"What I can tell you, young Courage, is that you have been given the gift to choose if you want to connect with humans, if you continue to do so, you must discern between the human with understanding and the human without, I can only guide you my son," his father had cautioned.

Chapter Three

Courage went into a dreamlike state, remembering that special day when his father revealed so much to him. The dreamy stallion slowly awakened as Adri repeatedly nudged him to move forward. "Courage, Courage, HELLO COURAGE!" Adri finally hollered and gave him a shove to bring him back to reality. "Courage! Move forward so we can find different grass!" she scolded the newly roused stallion.

Courage refocused his eyes on his father and mother grazing on the other side of the herd and then the memory hit him. He suddenly froze, his eyes went wide, and his tail went straight up. "Shalot! How could I forget about my dear friend Shalot?" he asked himself aloud. It was the first time he remembered that Shalot had been snatched from her family since that day he spoke to his father about her. Oh how he hoped she was safely home by now. He decided that he would have to find out…. Right Now! But, Boy oh BOY, Father would be so angry with him!

Courage slowly and deliberately maneuvered himself away from the herd. He made sure to keep one eye on his family, hoping his herd mates were not paying too close attention to him. He got far enough away, below a hill, where his herd could no longer see him. The exuberant stallion grinned and jumped into the air, "Woo Hoo!" he hollered with excitement as he turned toward the direction of his friend's home and took off at a trot. Courage eased into a nice soft canter, bucking, and kicking along the way, then the young energetic stallion chuckled and shouted with glee, "What am I doing? I LOVE to GO FAST!"

Young Courage galloped with all his might, playing all the way, running fast and hard up and down every hill he met. The warmer he became from his run, the more refreshing the cool air felt to him. Courage finally got to the top of the hill where he'd first met Mia and came to a screeching halt. The curious stallion surveyed the grounds to locate Mia, Shalot, or his human friend, Zander, but they were nowhere to be seen. He continued to keep a look out for his friends while his breathing returned to normal. Young Courage loudly purged the remaining adrenaline from his nostrils and shook his mane from side to side. "Whew, I am one HUN…GRY stallion!" he declared and started eating the newly grown grass, keeping one eye focused on his friend's home and one eye watching behind. *JUST IN CASE,* he thought.

Chapter Four

Zander walked out of the barn concentrating on the next job on his list, fixing fence. He didn't mind mending fence at all. It was a good break from his day. He looked down and realized he forgot the nails. He abruptly turned to go back to the barn and stopped cold when his eye caught movement on top of the hill. He focused in on the four-legged creature that stood more than 400 feet away from him and his heart welled up with excitement. "Is that YOU my friend?" he whispered. He squinted his eyes and sure enough, it was Courage. He recognized the long legs and brown coat. If the handsome stallion stood any closer he would be able to spot his doe-like eyes. Zander's eyes began to well up with tears and his heart was exploding with love and excitement. He wanted so much to jump up and down and holler at the top of his lungs, "COURAGE is BACK!!" Oh how he loved this brown stallion. It had been over eight weeks since he last saw him, and he thought of him all the time.

Zander awoke every morning thinking about Courage and fell asleep every night with this young stallion on his mind. He thought of him many, many times in between. He prayed for Courage as hard as he could and wished he would come back. He daydreamed about the times he rode the young stallion bareback, how great it felt when they galloped freely together and how it warmed his heart when Courage nuzzled him or when he trotted to meet him. He deeply missed his friend and now this stallion who stole his heart was back, looking as strong and brave as he did before he left to go back to his family. The tears in Zander's eyes finally welled up and trickled down his cheek, "Courage is back!" Zander expressed tenderly.

Zander moved slowly but deliberately back inside the barn to put his tools down. He grabbed a halter and lead rope just in case Courage wanted to partner up. Zander sauntered out of the barn and returned to the same spot. He looked over at Courage, and they locked eyes. Courage had moved toward him another fifty feet while he was in the barn. When Zander met the stallion's gaze he had to remember to breathe. His excitement was so high that his heart was beating out of his chest. "Breathe, Zander, Breathe!" he encouraged himself.

Courage's head was high, his neck looked tight from where he stood, and both ears and eyes were fixed on Zander. The boy waited for a sign that Courage wanted to connect with him. Courage would drop his head to the earth and grab a few blades of grass always keeping an eye on Zander, and then Courage's head would pop back up and watch Zander more intently. He continued to wait patiently for the young stallion to make a move in his direction. After some time, Zander noticed that Courage's head wouldn't spring up as fast or as high as it did only a few minutes before and his neck seemed much softer. "Good Boy.... just relax," Zander whispered with a smile. As he uttered the words, he wasn't quite sure if he was saying this to Courage or to himself.

Zander finally saw that Courage was much more relaxed, so he started to play a game with him. Whenever Courage was looking at him confidently, Zander would try to draw the young stallion to him, by taking slow deliberate steps backwards or turning and walking a few steps in the opposite direction. Whenever Courage got distracted and lost interest in Zander, he would walk assertively toward his tail and stop immediately when he regained the young stallion's attention. Sometimes, to draw the curious stallion's awareness he would do jumping jacks, cartwheels or even dance. *I really hope no one is watching me!* Zander said to himself and laughed.

Every time this inquisitive brave stallion gave Zander his attention, he would stop and ask him to be his partner once again by backing away. Zander played this game with Courage for what seemed like an hour but it was really only a quarter of that time. They managed to close the distance between each other by half. However, the young stallion was not yet confident in connecting with Zander, and the boy knew it. "Well my equine friend, everything means something and you just aren't ready yet... that's alright... I'll wait," Zander said aloud to Courage as if he were standing right next to him.

Zander squatted close to the ground, he picked up a few dandelions and blew on them, watching the seeds float in the air, parachuting slowly back to the earth that surrounded him. He breathed deeply and thought about how lucky he was to be able to play with horses and be amongst nature every single day. *Yes siree, he was blessed for sure,* he thought to himself. Zander continued to breathe deeply and think about his blessings rather than focus on Courage and then *IT HAPPENED*!

Chapter Five

Courage's overwhelming curiosity to find out if Shalot had returned home had grown into a fiery excitement that burned inside him. He had become more and more eager to reunite with his horse and human friends as he galloped toward their home. He had traveled the few miles feverishly, but when Zander appeared outside the barn the young stallion became immediately skeptical. Even though he knew and cared for this boy, his father's words troubled him and his instincts told him to be cautious. When the human boy kneeled to the ground, very quickly Courage felt less claustrophobic and less pressure from him. As his fear began to melt away he became more and more interested in what his human friend was doing. The young stallion's curiosity outweighed his skepticism, so he started slowly moving toward the boy. Courage cautiously stepped toward Zander, his head low, blowing out his nostrils and rhythmically breathing with each stride he made. It felt good to him. *Hmmm...what is my friend doing? Why did he stop playing with me?* He wondered. The curious stallion walked faster. *Is he sleeping? Is he eating?* Courage questioned. He continued walking toward his human friend until he got close enough to see what Zander was doing, but he still wasn't too sure that he was safe. The interested stallion snatched a couple blades of grass while he continued to watch the boy. As he eyed Zander, Courage blew out his nostrils and slowly walked toward him once again, inching closer until he was near enough to make contact with his human friend.

The young stallion stopped and blew out his nostrils with all his might. He slowly reached out his neck, and when his whiskers touched the boy's knee, he quickly recoiled his neck just enough to register what he had felt. Courage walked a few more steps, blew out his nostrils yet again and shook his mane really hard. *Whew, I feel really good! I like being here with this boy. I can tell my father that this human understands me... I just know he does,* he thought confidently. Courage touched Zander once again but this time on Zander's chin and then his ear, and then the top of his head. He started nodding and gave Zander a short nicker. *Yes, I do love this boy...he IS my friend, YES he IS!* Courage assured himself. He stretched his neck over the top of Zander, placing himself in just the right position to get his itchy spots scratched. *Scratch my itchy spots – please, please – please!* Courage silently begged. He didn't have to ask his friend again. Zander reached over and scratched all the right spots.

Chapter Six

Zander made sure he took a lot of time to scratch on Courage and young Courage enjoyed every minute of it. Zander just grinned, knowing how much this pleased his equine friend. The itchy stallion would lower his head and ask Zander to scratch closer to his withers, he would walk forward turn his hind end into Zander and back up. *"How about here, Please, Please, Please?"* Courage pleaded. Zander laughed and scratched Courage's rump and tail. He scratched and scratched and scratched, and Courage LOVED it! "I LOVE my itchy spots to be scratched!" the young delighted stallion exclaimed with pure joy.

Zander had spent a good half hour there on the hill with Courage, just talking to him and rubbing all his itchy spots. Zander told the young stallion all about how he and his Father went to countless events and auctions over the last eight weeks with no luck finding Shalot. "Courage, I just don't know where else to look, I'm at the end of my rope!" Zander said discouraged.

The confident Stallion backed away from the boy. He wasn't sure what Zander said to him, but he could feel the energy change. It was negative and depressing, and if this was about their friend Shalot he was not going to have any of it! Courage started snorting and pawing the ground with a few half rears. "We are going to find Shalot! I am here with you now and I KNOW we will find her, YOU can't give up, WE can do this together!" Courage expressed persuasively, delivering another half rear and a buck for effect.

Zander watched Courage with both awe and amusement. "You don't want us to give up, do you boy?" he asked the sensitive stallion. Courage snorted and threw his head, shaking his mane vigorously. Zander laughed heartily at his four-legged friend's dramatic gestures. "Ok, ok. You're right! We both have the heart and desire, so we will make it OUR mission to find Shalot!" Zander exclaimed with so much passion and enthusiasm that it triggered Courage's excitement.

Courage jumped as high as he could with all four feet in the air, he ran around in a circle, bucked, played, and snaked his head to the left. "Woo Hoo!" Then Courage snaked his head to the right "We are going to find our friend Shalot, oh yes we are, oh yes we ARE!" Courage sang and pranced. Then he stopped cold and blew out his nostrils. "But boy, OH BOY, father is going to be very angry with me!" he uttered to himself.

Chapter Seven

Zander decided right then and there that they WOULD find Shalot, and he wasn't going to think otherwise ever again! He was always amazed at how deep his learning could be with horses and his four-legged friend just helped him absorb the true meaning of COURAGE!

When things seem stacked against me, causing me to doubt myself, causing me not to believe in myself .... I have to have COURAGE! Zander thought as he allowed the concept to unfold in his head and heart. After several seconds Zander spoke aloud slowly and deliberately, "No matter how difficult things may seem and no matter what others tell me I should do or believe. I have to have courage. YES! I HAVE TO HAVE COURAGE to follow my heart and – well – to BELIEVE in ME, to follow through in what I BELIEVE! I HAVE to have COURAGE!" Zander bellowed, feeling inspired and blessed. "Thank you my friend for helping me see!" he said to young Courage. The sensitive stallion watched his human friend as he grazed, feeling his energy shift, which was relaxing to him and caused him to blow out any remaining anxiety from his nostrils.

With Zander's newly discovered meaning of the word courage, he hung the halter and lead rope over the inside of his elbow. "Forget about the halter, my friend, let's see what the truth says about our connection. I have courage buddy boy. Do YOU?" Zander asked Courage. He gave the itchy stallion one last scratch, took a deep breath, looked at the barn and began moving very slowly toward it. He hoped Courage would stay connected to him as they walked, but he knew the horse might turn tail and run.   Zander looked over and smiled brightly as the pair strolled together in harmony the last 100 feet to the barn.

As they grew near their destination, Courage became more and more concerned. They passed by a piece of wood leaning against the wall, Courage snorted and moved away quickly, watching the piece of timber to see if it would eat him. *What in the world is that?* He wondered to himself. The pair approached a few long round objects lying on the ground. Courage could not quite figure out what they were, so the unconfident stallion began snorting and prancing. *Where did all these new, scary things come from?* He thought to himself as he abruptly stopped and backed several feet to look at the spooky objects more closely and to make certain they didn't make a move toward him.

Zander observed the young stallion and grinned. "Come on Courage, you can get through this can't you?" the boy asked teasingly. They finally got past the poles that Zander used for jumps and walked slowly into the barn.

Courage let out a long sigh… "It's about time! Now things are starting to look like I remember!" he exclaimed with relief. Then he saw Mia. She stood in the same stall as before, when she had nursed Courage back to health. The excited stallion left the boy's side and rushed into the stall where he used to stand right next to the loving mare. "Yep, still the same in here!" he exclaimed.

"Courage! Oh Courage, I am so happy to see you! You have grown so much in just a few short months." Mia said cheerfully.

Zander left the stall door open so Courage could come and go as he wanted. Zander made up a pan of grain, grabbed a flake of hay and set them inside the door for the young stallion. Both Mia and Courage were nickering to each other and obviously happy so he tended to a few other chores in the barn while they reunited. "Thank you ma'am, I mean Mia." Courage answered politely.

"We missed you around here, especially Zander, he talks about you ALL the time!" she told Courage.

"What does he say, Miss Mia?" he asked curiously.

"Well, he can't stop talking about what a brave stallion you are and how you saved your sister from being snatched by the same bad man that abducted Shalot. Oh my dear Shalot," Mia painfully sighed.

"Mia – I am so sorry that Shalot is still missing. But I am back now and the human boy and I are going to find her. We have made it our – our mission to find Shalot and I assure you Mia we will find her in no time!" Courage said confidently as he puffed out his chest.

Mia dropped her head as the sadness of Shalot's absence overcame her. She wanted to believe her friend, Courage, but it had been so long, would they really have a chance of finding her sweet filly? She hung her head low and went somewhere deep inside herself, a place where she didn't have to think about her little filly or feel her heart hurt.

Courage could feel Mia's tremendous pain and deep sadness. The young stallion stood quietly beside the heartbroken mare for a long while, hoping she would feel his comfort and love. He wanted her to feel assured that *he and his human friend, Zander, would find Shalot, Oh yes they would!* Courage thought to himself. There was no doubt in his mind, and now there was only sheer determination!

Chapter Eight

Zander left Courage's stall open, allowing him the choice to return to the wild if he wanted. Every so often, Zander came into the barn and checked on the young stallion, who was either eating or standing next to Mia. Zander decided to take a quick break and go inside his home to eat a sandwich and tell his parent's all about his morning with Courage, but his parents were not home. Zander pinched his own arm to convince himself that this was really happening, "OUCH!" he jumped. "Yep, it sure is!" he grinned as he swooped up his boots and made his way back outside to see about his young friend. As he put his boots on his feet, he delighted in the beauty of the day, not a cloud in the sky, nice and warm, just the way he liked it. Zander slowly stood up and stretched his arms to the sky and started to make his way to the barn, he instantly stopped when he saw a sight that made him giggle. Courage was inside the arena, going from one obstacle to the next, checking each of them out in great detail. Zander sat down on the swing outside the bay window of their home and observed the curious stallion.

Courage looked up, saw Zander and decided to encourage his friend to come play with him. The playful stallion had checked out all the objects in the arena and they were the same as he remembered. Courage sprung into a trot then looked back at Zander who was now sitting on the porch behind Courage. "Come on! Let's pick up where we left off!" the exuberant stallion whinnied to the grinning boy. He looked down at the barrels that stood about 2 feet tall and jumped them. He turned, looked back at Zander once again and saw the boy smiling. *OK, let's see if this works!* Courage thought.

The lively stallion bounced into a trot. As he approached the long object that humans call a bridge, he slowed to a walk then stopped in front of it. He dropped his head to get a better feel for the bridge then slowly reached his neck over it and stepped his front right foot onto it, then his left front foot. He looked back at Zander for a response, but all he saw was a smile on Zander's face and no movement in his direction. Courage licked and chewed and confidently said to himself, *Yep, just how I remember it!* Courage slowly walked all four of his feet onto the bridge, found the center and stood there feeling extremely pleased with himself. He turned to look at his friend once again, hoping he was on his way to come play with him, but Zander just stood motionless with his mouth open and in silence. *Hmm – this is not what I am looking for! What is it going to take to get this boy to come play with me?* He thought with annoyance. He slowly walked off the bridge and decided to go push that big ball around. *That was always fun!* He thought. Courage walked over to the ball and pushed it with his nose and looked at Zander once again. "We have to get going so we can find Shalot, come on – come on – COME ON!" He called to Zander as he snaked his head, picked up a trot and rolled the ball around the arena.

Zander chuckled, walked toward the arena and stopped as he watched Courage. The determined stallion stopped and said assertively, "That's it? Come on! We can't waste any time!" Courage then remembered the pattern that Zander and he did when the boy was on his back. *Maybe this will do it!* He thought to himself as he walked in a circle half a lap, trotted two laps, cantered one lap, walked half a lap and stopped. He looked at Zander as Zander walked toward him once again. "Woo Hoo! I'm a big..." he sang as he walked. "I am a BAD," he sang as he picked up a trot. "I am a BRAVE stallion!" he continued to sing as he bounded into a canter. "And I LOVE to go FAST!" he bellowed as he accelerated into a gallop and came to a sliding stop. Courage backed up a few steps, sighed, blew out his nostrils and looked at Zander as the boy walked into the arena.

"Whew! It's about time! I was running out of ideas!" Courage exclaimed as he watched Zander approach slowly then stop short of walking all the way to meet him. The young impatient stallion was having none of that. They needed to keep moving along. They had a mission – A mission to find Shalot with all their heart and desire! Courage walked the rest of the way to Zander, shook his mane hard and nuzzled Zander and nickered.

Zander was pleasantly surprised at how quickly they were falling into their herd of two again, how quick the connection renewed and how willing Courage was to be Zander's partner once again. He decided to just feel for it. "Well, you're obviously ready to pick up where we left off, huh boy?" he asked the eager stallion. The stallion nodded as if he understood Zander's question. Zander laughed, gave Courage a rub, and with one fell swoop, Zander was up on Courage's back. Zander rubbed Courage on his mane, between his ears, on his hind end and then he asked Courage to walk forward.

Both Zander and Courage heard vehicles approaching and saw that Zander's father, Mark, and his mother, Rachel, pulled up in the family truck with another truck following. The boy and the young stallion were aware of their surroundings but were much more focused on reconnecting with each other and preparing for their mission… to bring Shalot home!

Chapter Nine

"Rachel, are you seeing what I'm seeing?" Mark asked in utter surprise.

"I can't believe it, Courage is back!" Rachel answered in total disbelief. They got out of the truck and stood next to the vehicle as they watched their son and the young stallion walk and trot around the arena.

Lowell, a local racehorse owner, well known for his integrity, love for horses, and winning big races got out of his truck and made his way over to where they were standing. Lowell and Mark had been friends since they were in elementary school. He had a training facility a mile down the road and tried to have lunch with Mark every now and again – which is where they had been today.

As they watched the young pair play together, Rachel filled Lowell in on the story of Courage. She explained how this young stallion had appeared out of nowhere and in such a short period of time, saved the day time and time again. She described how the brave stallion chose to go back into the wild with his herd after he saved his sister and father from the man who had abducted their very own filly, Shalot. The endearing stallion had been gone ever since, and none of them was really sure that he would ever return.

They watched their son riding the energetic stallion in the arena. Every once in- awhile, Courage would give a playful buck, some a bit more dramatic than others. Sometimes Courage would bear down and gallop faster than Zander was asking, but the boy would just relax, grin and ride through those moments. They walked, trotted and jumped over barrels and poles, walked over a small bridge Mark had made out of wood and over a couple different sized tarps. When Zander asked Courage for a lope, the sensitive young stallion easily went into the requested gait – around and around they went, gliding effortlessly like they had been doing this everyday. Zander had a big smile on his face, and if they didn't know any better, they would say Courage did too.

"Woo Hoo, I LOVE to go FAST!" the energetic stallion exclaimed. Zander asked Courage to come to a stop at the center of the arena, and he responded instantaneously by smoothly gliding to a halt. Zander fondly rubbed the respectful young stallion's neck, rewarded him with a treat and allowed young Courage to rest.

Mark, Rachel and Lowell approached the arena to greet Zander, and the boy could not wait to share with them what had transpired that morning with the young stallion. He began passionately recounting the details of his morning: how he noticed young Courage on the hill, how they reconnected, and the playful stallion's dramatic gestures in the arena.

As the boy cheerfully spoke, young Courage rested with one eye on his friend, Zander, and the other eye cautiously on the new human that was with the boy's parents. This man seemed okay to Courage, but he would DEFINITELY pay close attention to him JUST IN CASE he was one of those humans that didn't respect his kind. Courage blew out his nostrils and nodded his head as he rested.

Lowell was a tall, lean man, with once light brown hair now starting to gray. He listened to Zander's story and smiled. "Son, your parents were telling me about your history with Courage and your natural talent and abilities with horses," Lowell complimented the boy. "I was wondering if you would like to come out and break a little filly of mine. She is strong and well-bred for racing and she looks to me like she could really have something. With that said, she is pretty hard to handle, we got her from a sale a month ago, and she has given all the handlers a run for their money. I think you just might be the ticket to help her get a solid shot at showing her talent. What do you say?" Lowell asked Zander.

"Well sir, my grandfather Jackson, taught me that starting horses is one of the most beautiful gifts a human could be given. He believed in the approach of giving them a connection to us in a positive partnering way rather than breaking their spirit by making them do what we humans want them to do. Sir, if you are good with me *starting* rather than *breaking* her, I'll certainly help you and the filly out," Zander responded respectfully.

Young Courage cocked his head to the side, recognizing the name Jackson from the discussion with his father. The sleepy stallion didn't understand anything else that was said. He stomped his foot and resumed relaxing.

Lowell grinned at the young stallion and responded to Zander's question with a gentle laugh. "I sure am son. I was fortunate enough to witness your Granddad over the years start quite a few young horses. I was always impressed by how gentle but firm his feel was with those colts and son that old man sure did have perfect timing to help those colts learn. His connection to those horses, well… let's just say there wasn't one of those horses that didn't just love him."

Lowell paused, and with another laugh he continued, "I laugh only because your Grandfather Jackson would correct me when I used the term "break" just as you did. He was always very particular in the words he used because he said it translated into actions. So, yes son, this is going to be quite the treat having his methods applied to this little filly, and I'm very interested in how all this might help her in her development as a racehorse. Heck, who really knows what this could all turn into!" Lowell said proudly.

Zander was pleased that Lowell wanted a good positive start for the little filly, and had one more order of business to clear up.

"Sir, there is one other thing, Courage and I have a priority and that is to find Shalot, our missing filly. So, both Courage and I will make that our mission to find her as soon as possible," Zander declared.

"Well, I am supportive of that, and I'll do whatever I can to help you son." Lowell said with a wink.

26

"Thank you, Sir, I'll come out to your place later today if that's alright?" Zander asked. He dismounted Courage and walked over to the arena railing to extend his hand to Lowell.

"I'm looking forward to it," Lowell replied as he shook Zander's hand, turned and headed back to his truck.

"Well, son, it looks like you are going to be one busy young man!" Mark said proudly.

Zander smiled and suddenly felt Courage's presence and breath over his shoulder. The young devoted stallion had followed him to the side of the arena, nuzzling the boy, wanting nothing more than to be with his human friend. This act of love warmed Zander's heart.

Chapter Ten

A few hours later Zander gathered a few of his horseman tools from
the barn: his rope halter, lead rope, flag and horse treats and turned
to see what Courage was doing. The peaceful stallion was standing in
the aisle adjacent to Mia's stall, both of them side by side with only a
partition separating them. Both horses were very relaxed and quiet.
Zander turned to walk out of the barn. He planned to have his father
drive him over to Lowell's ranch and leave him there for a few hours.
Zander walked toward the truck, deep in thought, pondering what
the next step should be to find their friend, Shalot. He heard footfalls
behind him, so he slowed his pace and felt Courage's breath on his
neck. He slowly turned, and there stood his four-legged friend.

I am going with you, Courage thought confidently as he nodded
and shook his mane. Zander looked into this passionate stallion's
eyes and knew he wanted to go along with him. Courage had never
been saddled so Zander stood there contemplating what he should
do. The boy suddenly smiled widely, turned and jogged back to the
barn, with the willing young stallion trotting right by his side.
Zander had prepared young Courage with a bare back pad in a few of
his sessions before he left a few months ago, so today that was what
they would ride in.

Zander hugged Courage's body with the pad a few times, letting
him feel the foreign object on his back. The brave stallion accepted
it as if there was never a lapse in time from several weeks earlier.
Zander took his time cinching up the pad to see if Courage had any
issues with the strap around his belly.

Don't treat me like a baby – we've done this already, the comfortable but impatient stallion thought as he sighed.

Zander moved young Courage around. Indeed he was relaxed and calm with the pad over his back and the cinch under his belly. Zander packed his tools into a backpack, threw the pack onto his back, grinned at his determined partner and agreeably said, "OK boy, you want to go…. Let's go!" He mounted the young stallion, and Courage immediately looked up at his friend with his right eye, seeking reassurance. Zander rubbed the young stallion's neck, rubbed between his ears, gave him a treat and off they went.

As they trotted along the path, Courage hunted the ground, exploring his surroundings. All of a sudden he saw something swaying in the breeze and stopped cold, almost frozen, his head up, neck tight, and his eyes wide as silver dollars. Zander talked to him and just waited until the stallion relaxed and moved forward again. *I'm a big, I'm a brave – I am a BIG BRAVE Stallion! Yes, I AM! I MUST be if I am to find Shalot!* Courage repeated to himself. He blew out his nostrils, shook his head, blinked his eyes and then started moving forward again. Zander would just grin and off they would go at a trot.

They came to an open field, that led to Lowell's property and Zander wondered if the enthusiastic stallion would pick up a lope. Zander decided to ask Courage to trot faster to see how he would respond. The spirited stallion answered the boy by lowering his head and offering the most rounded, magnificent canter Zander had ever rode. They loped and loped and loped, with the breeze on their faces and an overwhelming feeling of satisfaction and fulfillment. It was so beautiful and powerful for both horse and human to feel this strong connection when they both had the same idea, the same desire, and the same rhythm. *This is harmony!* thought Zander.

They slowed when they arrived at Lowell's ranch, admiring the large, gold plated entrance. The pair made their way through the gate, amazed with the beauty, sophistication and neatness of the facility. They walked slowly toward the barn and then suddenly they were both struck by the smoke coming from somewhere beyond Lowell's ranch.

Chapter Eleven

Courage's head shot straight up at the very moment that Zander noticed the smoke. "That does not look good my friend!" Zander said with great concern. Courage was very still, eyes locked on the smoke in the distance; and his neck and body were tight.

What is that? Courage wondered.

"Let's make our way over there, boy, and see what we can do to help," Zander said confidently to the young stallion as he encouraged him to pick up a trot. They jogged through the lanes surrounded by paddocks of horses.

Courage hadn't seen things like this before, and he was curious, worried and sometimes downright scared. Courage dodged a water hose that looked like a snake. He jumped in place at a half barrel filled with water, *Whoa! What is that?* Courage asked himself. When they came upon horse blankets hanging on a fence, blowing erratically from the strong breeze, Courage snorted loudly, planted his front feet on the ground both eyes and ears locked on the objects, then he impulsively started running backwards. *What is that? I am a big, I am a brave – Yikes! What is that? I am a big brave stallion, yes, yes I am!* He kept repeating over and over to encourage himself.

Zander stroked Courage's neck to reassure him that all was okay as they were backing up through the laneway at a fast pace. Courage barely felt Zander's touch as he only thought of Survival. *This is too much! I can't – I can't process all of this without taking a minute to think!* Courage cried.

Zander talked softly to the young scared stallion, staying loose and riding whatever Courage presented to him. "It's all ok, boy. No worries, it's just a blanket, Courage. It looks bad up ahead, a whole lot worse than a horse blanket, my friend. I need you to think. Come on boy, just try to think." Zander kept encouraging his fearful stallion friend.

Courage finally stopped when he felt he was at a safe distance from the moving object, he intently observed it, and blew out his nostrils really loud and shook his head and mane hard. He watched the blanket once again. After a few minutes he slowly started approaching it. Courage walked a few steps, stopped, and focused intently on the blanket. He walked a few more steps, stopped, stared at the blanket once again, and looked back at Zander periodically to feel his energy.

Courage decided that there was nothing to be frightened of, so he inched closer and closer to the blanket yet again. He very slowly and cautiously reached out his neck, touched his nose to the blanket and quickly recoiled. *That wasn't so bad,* he thought to himself. He blinked and reached out his neck once again, touching the scary object this time a little harder, pushing and lifting it with his nose.

Young Courage then grabbed onto the blanket with his teeth and started flailing it around. *Woo Hoo, I've got it, Ha, Ha!* He said to himself. Bit by bit the blanket came loose from the rail, and as he tugged on it the stallion noticed the scary object moving toward him. Courage immediately backed away then he backed faster, "YIKES!" He screamed with his teeth tightly clamped onto the blanket. The faster Courage ran backwards the faster the object chased him! "OHHHHHHHH – NOOO!!!!! Courage screamed as he finally let go of the blanket, and it immediately fell to the ground and stopped moving. Courage continued to move backward for a few more steps, and then he realized it stopped. "Whew!" he exclaimed as he finally stopped cold and stared wide eyed at the blanket.

He blew out his nostrils and shook his head, walked forward cautiously just in case this thing started chasing him again, but as he approached, it did not move. He again pushed it around with his nose, and there was no response. He blew out loudly, allowing all of the pent-up anxiety to scatter from his nostrils! *What a relief, it is dead!* He said to himself. *I am a big brave stallion, Oh YES I AM!* He said proudly to himself as he continued to blow out his nostrils and stomp on the blanket.

Zander couldn't help but laugh. Courage continued to let go of all that fear he was harboring inside, and Zander just waited for him to gain his confidence once again. Then finally when Zander asked Courage to move forward he did with assurance, "I am A BIG, BRAVE Stallion! Oh YES I am!" he sang as he pranced along.

Courage confidently strutted down the lane surrounded by vacant pens. As they neared the end of the laneway, a miniature painted mule trotted toward them on the other side of the fence. "WHOA!!!! What in the WORLD is THAT?" Courage cried loudly, and he was NOT about to stick around to find out! His body faced forward to run away, but the boy asked him to keep looking at the small four-legged creature with gigantic ears. Courage panicked and tried to run as fast as he could! "Let's get out of here!" Courage shrieked.

The fearful young stallion wanted to do nothing more than move away from the mule as fast as he possibly could. Zander allowed Courage to move his feet and drift away from the mule, but he kept the scared stallion's head and neck bent toward the mule so that Courage would move sideways rather than forward. This gave the worried horse both time and distance to figure out that this mule wasn't going to hurt him.

Courage stood frozen in fear, his eyes wide and locked on this short painted animal, his ears were forward and his whole body was extremely tight. "Come on, PLEASE – let's go!" Courage said as he tried to turn and run once again but Zander kept him facing the mule.

Zander wanted to get to the fire as soon as he was able, but his priority at hand was developing young Courage's confidence so Zander continued to patiently reassure him.

"Come on boy you can figure this out. You've got COURAGE, you can do it!" It seemed like they stood motionless for five minutes or more before the fearful stallion finally lowered his head and took a step toward her.

The cute little mule stuck her head through the fence trying to reach Courage, which made the skeptical stallion more and more curious. "What in the world is this spotted thing?" Courage asked puzzled.

"Well… I'm not a thing!" the miniature mule responded with annoyance.

Courage was shocked that she answered him.

"Um – you can hear me?" he asked her.

"Of course, silly. I'm not a thing! I am a mule, a short and cute one at that!" she said sharply. "My name is Korin, what is your name, young man?" she asked.

"My name is Courage!" the stallion responded proudly.

"Ha, Ha, Ha, HA, HA! Your name is Cour–age?" Korin continued to laugh hysterically. "Son, YOU DID NOT look so COURAGEous to me, running from that blanket!" she chuckled and continued. "And if that wasn't enough – trying to turn tail and run from a cute little thing like me!" she teased.

Courage got a sour look on his face from her sarcasm, "Well, I've never seen things like this and – and – the blanket scared me, and well – I'm still confused, as to what YOU ARE?" he replied with hurt feelings.

"There's nothing much you need to be scared of around here, son. As for me, well, I am like you, but I have a different father called a donkey – I get my long ears from him. I tend to be bossy, short, and loving all at that same time!" she said with a wink and a laugh.

Courage took a step in the sassy mule's direction, slowly reaching his nose toward her. Korin reached out her nose to make contact with the inexperienced stallion and swiftly nipped him on the chin. Courage pinned his ears and charged the fence.

Zander laughed. "You trying to show her whose boss?" Zander teased with a chuckle.

Courage shook his head, snorted and eyed Korin. "That wasn't very nice!" he scolded as he lowered his head and stared into her eyes.

"I told you I was bossy! See you around, YOUNG Cour–age!" she teased laughing all the way back to her hay. Courage shook his head and watched the funny looking miniature mule walk away.

The young stallion continued to stand there for another minute shaking his head and mane, finally relaxed enough for them to move forward. Once they took a few steps forward, Courage focused on the commotion ahead. The duo picked up a trot. When they came to open pasture, they bounded into a canter and then transitioned smoothly into a gallop! "Woo Hoo! I LOVE to go fast!" Courage sang as they raced toward the neighbors in need and Zander just smiled.

Chapter Twelve

As Zander and Courage got closer to the smoke, they could see that a barn was engulfed in an angry fire burning out of control. The pair approached the small crowd gathered near the barn. Zander swiftly jumped off the young stallion's back, and he cautiously approached an older woman whose long gray hair was neatly pulled away from her face by a braid. The woman stood motionless watching the fire with her arms crossed and tears rolling down her face. "Ma'am, is there anything we can do to help?" Zander asked her gently.

"Oh son, the firemen are doing the best they can, trying to save this old place. I don't know if there is anything else that can be done right now but wait." She replied with a catch in her voice.

"Ma'am, was there livestock in the barn?" Zander asked hoping the answer would be no.

The lady swallowed hard and wiped the tears from her eyes. "Not in the barn, but there was a filly and my mare in the paddock next to the barn. They got scared, jumped the fence and ran toward the tree line over there. She pointed in the general direction of their path. My granddaughter and her granddaddy are on our four-wheeler trying to locate them." she replied with great concern in her voice.

"Well ma'am, maybe that is what Courage and I can do to help, we can look for the mare and filly and bring them back. If that would be all right with you?" Zander asked the fragile woman.

The woman turned and for the first time saw the young, dark, handsome stallion standing next to the boy. She gasped. "Oh, my!

What a handsome horse!" she exclaimed. "Yes, that would be so wonderful if you both could manage to look for them. Thank you, thank you so very much! By the way, my name is Debra, Debra Bates," she said as she reached out her hand to shake Zander's.

Zander put his hand in hers and formally introduced himself. "Hi Debra, I'm Zander and this here is my partner, Courage." Debra smiled and for the first time, Zander noticed this woman's piercing green eyes with faint wrinkles at the corners. He could see the years of love and wisdom reflecting back to him. Zander jumped up on Courage's back. "Ma'am, I mean, Debra, one more thing. What do the horses look like?" Zander asked.

"My mare is as white as they come and very tall, a little over 16 hands – and well – the filly is really new to us. Hillary, my granddaughter, found her roaming in the backfield, we are pretty sure she was abandoned by – well that's a long story. Anyway, she is red with a gold mane and a white stripe down her nose, she's quite thin, too thin, and it looks like she has been beat up a bit," Debra explained thoughtfully. "Hillary is a city girl and doesn't know much about horses, but fell immediately in love with this little filly." she said with a smile.

Zander's eyes grew big. "Courage, I think we may have found our Shalot!" Zander hollered with pure joy. Courage recognized the excited energy in his friend's voice when he heard Shalot's name and he was eager to follow Zander's lead so they took off as fast as they could go. Both boys' hearts were pounding and racing in hopes that this could be their Shalot!

Debra looked puzzled as the boy and Courage left on their mission. She repeated the name the boy had spoken, "Shalot?" She was truly bewildered as she turned back to the blazing storm of fire in front of her. "Oh my!" she muttered as she watched everyone working diligently to put out the flames.

Chapter Thirteen

Zander and Courage trotted along the path that they believed the two horses may have taken into the forest. When the pair reached the tree line and slowed to a stop, each took on a job. Courage called loudly to his horse friend while Zander explored different options for them to enter into the woods. They could hear an ATV in the distance. Then they heard the frantic horses return Courage's call. Courage bellowed back to the frightened horses, "We are coming! Keep talking to us!"

Courage was ready to get moving, so he started pawing. *Come on Zander, follow me!* He thought.

Zander could feel Courage welling up with power and the need to go forward, so Zander dropped the reins, grabbed a bit of mane and said, "Ok boy, it's all yours… FIND THEM!"

When Courage felt Zander let go of the reins, he was so proud that his friend trusted and believed in him that it helped Courage feel like such a big, brave stallion! Courage trotted through the path between the trees with his head down to the ground following the girl's route. The pair continued to move forward and ever so often Courage would stop and call and the lost horses would call back. Courage knew in his heart it was Shalot. They could still hear the ATV in the distance but it sounded like it was going in a different direction than they were traveling. The sun would soon set and Zander was hoping they would find the horses before dark.

Courage was the bravest he had ever been and he was thankful to his human friend for taking the time to help him through his fear.

Now he didn't let the sounds behind the trees, the shadows that followed them or the rustling of the leaves bother him. *No Sirree, we are on a mission to find Shalot and nothing will stop us!* Courage thought to himself. They traveled another half mile, following a path that Courage was sure the horses were on when Courage heard the mare call to him.

"Hello, young man, can you hear me?" the mare called.

"Yes, yes, Ma'am. I can hear you. My human friend and I are trying to find you," Courage replied.

"Is your name Courage?" the mare asked.

Courage was surprised. "Why, yes Ma'am, my name is Courage. How did you know?" he asked bewildered.

"Oh, goodness! We are so relieved! I will explain when we meet. We'll start toward you. Thank you, thank you so much for coming to find us, we are so scared!" she cried.

"Ma'am, please call to me along the way so we know we are on the same path," Courage asked the mare.

Zander knew the horses were communicating with each other as Courage trotted along with his head low to the ground following the scent and path of the horses. They continued to call to each other and with every turn in the path, they knew they were getting closer. When Zander finally heard their footfalls, they went around one more bend and there they were!

Chapter Fourteen

Zander could not believe his eyes. By the white mare's side stood Shalot. She looked as if she had lost a hundred pounds. She seemed weak, and her coat and eyes were dull.

Although Shalot didn't have much energy after the long, scary run, she was noticeably full of joy to see both of her friends. Zander jumped off of Courage's back, and Shalot immediately left the mare's side to meet the young stallion nose-to-nose. The pair stayed there for a while before Shalot reared and gave a little high-pitched scream. Courage danced and pranced and then they nuzzled each other once again.

Zander and the mare happily stood back and watched the two become reacquainted. Zander hoped that Shalot would be happy to see him as well. Shalot blew out her nostrils several times, lowered her head and then turned her gaze toward Zander. "Hello my pretty girl," he said to Shalot with a tear in his eye. Zander slowly backed a step to draw Shalot to him. She watched for a moment, blinked, lowered her head even more and took a few steps toward him. "I missed you so much baby girl!" he said to her.

She walked faster, her eyes and ears locked on her human friend and she trotted the rest of the way to greet him. He put his hand out palm face down to see if she wanted to get a rub. She touched the back of his hand letting him know it was okay. Zander smiled warmly at Shalot, and she responded by bumping his hand with her nose to flip his palm over. She licked and licked his palm. *Oh, how she missed her human friend and her mother!* She slowly took a step toward Zander, lifted and placed her head over his shoulder, nuzzling the boy.

"You giving me a hug pretty girl?" he asked her with a tear rolling down his cheek. He rubbed her neck and shoulders slowly as they remained in this affectionate embrace. She blew out her nostrils and took a step back.

Zander dug some treats out of his jeans' pocket and gave them to the horses.

"Shalot knew it was you!" the mare said to Courage with a smile.

"And I knew it was Shalot." the young proud stallion responded peacefully. They could still hear the four-wheeler, but it was at a distance.

"I think we ought to get back home to sort all this out before it gets dark. What do you all think?" Zander asked his four legged friends.

Young Courage blew out his nostrils, dropped his head and walked up to the boy. Zander gave the young stallion a rub and mounted him.

The boy and the faithful stallion picked up a trot and the girls followed closely behind. Zander wasn't sure if they would stay as a herd with Courage and himself, but he wanted to give it a try. The boy was pleased that he could feel the horses right there with them. They were traveling as one unit as fast as they could on the tight path through the woods.

Finally the trees opened up, and they found themselves in plain view of the burning barn. The once beautiful sky was filled with smoke. Zander checked his herd and saw that they all were relaxed and waiting for the next move. He decided they would trot until they got about 500 yards away from the barn and would walk the rest of the way in. They picked up a trot and started back to the mare's home.

Hillary and her grandfather were parked on their four-wheeler at the edge of the woods, but they were about a half a mile from where Zander and the herd made their exit out of the trees. "Grandpa, do you see that?" Hillary asked in total disbelief.

"Yes, Hilly I do see that!" Grandpa Phil responded. They saw the boy on the beautiful dark horse riding peacefully with the rescued horses on each side. "What a beautiful sight to behold! A boy and a herd of horses in harmony – it is just plain rare to see something like this anymore!" Grandpa Phil said to his granddaughter in awe. They continued to sit there for a moment forgetting all about the barn fire, immersing themselves in the beauty of horse and human trotting in harmony.

"Granddad, aren't we going to catch up with them?" Hillary asked impatiently.

"I don't think so, I think we'll take the back way in. Enjoy the view my girl," he answered his granddaughter with a wink. They continued to sit in silence and watch the boy and the horses make their way back home.

It touched Hillary's heart and filled her with such joy and love that this kind of connection was possible with these beautiful animals and she couldn't wait to get home and hug the little filly!

Courage arrived at the clearing and slowed down. The smoke was thick and pungent, and it bothered his eyes and nose. He didn't want to go any farther, and he could feel that the girls were nervous. "I think we should wait here," Courage said as he slowed to a stop.

Zander felt Courage and the girls' reluctance and allowed them to stop and rest. He just rubbed the three of them for a few minutes while he tried to figure out what was happening at the barn. Through the thick cloud of smoke, Zander could barely make out the firemen talking to Debra, and the four-wheeler slowly approaching the barn. When Zander considered asking the herd to move forward, Courage got extremely tight throughout his body, and Zander knew it wasn't just the smoke.

Chapter Fifteen

Courage spotted him! Hiding behind the trees, stood the man that had kidnapped Shalot! Courage not only saw him, but he smelled him too. He would recognize this bad human anywhere. Courage got agitated, and he became increasingly protective over his herd as he kept the evil human in his sight. Shalot grazed a few feet away from Courage, and he was afraid this man might see Shalot, so Courage turned and backed into her to move her out of the man's range of sight.

Well, that was rude! Shalot thought as she swished her tail at Courage.

Courage continued to get very tense and tight and Zander took notice. "What is it boy?" he asked. He followed Courage's focus and saw exactly why Courage was tight, and he was right – it wasn't the smoke!

Zander studied the man as best he could with the smoke thick in the air. He was definitely the man that had stolen Shalot, and luckily he had not seen their little herd that stood about 200 feet behind him. The man was hidden behind the trees and had his full attention on the commotion down by the barn. Zander felt Courage's tension beneath him and assessed the situation as quickly as he could before the man fled.

Young Courage knew that he had to do something so this bad man would not get away. He turned to the tall white mare and asked her for help. "Ma'am, I need you to help us out if you don't mind? There is a bad man hiding in those trees – the kind of human that my father said we ALWAYS should stay away from. I need you to keep Shalot calm and here with you – no matter what happens. Please, please, PLEASE stay far away from him! If you need to, take Shalot to your human friends. But never, I mean NEVER go near that man!"

She eyed the man and nodded. "My name is Eva and don't worry, you can count on me Courage!" she said reassuringly and gave the protective stallion a promising nod.

The unwavering young stallion tightened up like a coil, slowly and purposely giving his human friend warning. *I hope you are ready, because we are going!* Courage thought as he looked up at Zander with his right eye to see if he was with him.

Zander knew exactly what Courage was thinking; they were going to finish their mission. Zander quickly grabbed Courage's mane, gave him a reassuring rub and whispered, "Let's go finish this, boy!" The pair took off from a stand still into a gallop, headed full speed toward the man. They both were in unison and extremely focused on making sure this horrible man did not have an opportunity to flee.

Courage repeated to himself as he got closer and closer, *I am a brave, I am a very brave, I am a big, brave and strong stallion, and I am NOT going to let this man get away again! No sirree!* Courage and Zander ran with speed and determination. As they got closer they knew the man would hear the thunder of the stallion's hoofbeats, so they needed to be quick and accurate. They were only a few seconds away when the hidden man turned slowly to see what was behind him and Courage immediately sprung into action, forcing his shoulder into the surprised man and knocking him all at once to the ground. *There is NO WAY that YOU are getting away again… No Sirree..!* Courage thought loudly.

Zander leaped off of Courage, dropped squarely onto the man, tackling and pinning him to the ground. The man was strong and it took every ounce of mental and physical strength the boy had to hold the large man down and Zander wasn't quite sure how long he could hold him.

Courage slowed to a trot, changed his focus and headed to the crowd by the barn. *OH BOY, am I really going to run over to a bunch of humans and into this smoke?* Courage asked himself. *I am a big, I am a brave, I am a BIG, BRAVE stallion!* He repeated to himself. As he neared the crowd gathered by the barn, he started rearing to get their attention then he ran in circles and stopped to see if they were looking at him. Sure enough they were! He blew out his nostrils hard and loud for effect and threw his head in the direction of his friend. "Please, PLEASE come help!" Courage bellowed. The determined stallion reared and kicked in place continuing to invite the humans to come with him, and they finally started to understand.

"Oh my lands, that's Zander's young stallion! Where is Zander? It's like – like – this horse is trying to tell us something!" Debra said frantically to the people standing around her. Only seconds ago the concerned bystanders were captivated by the barn fire and now they stood in awe of this young stallion and his puzzling dramatic actions.

Hillary was certainly interested in what Courage was communicating, but she was more concerned about the little filly and Eva. Hillary looked back in the direction where the herd stood just a few minutes earlier and saw Eva and the little filly hadn't moved and were frozen in fear. Hillary immediately took off running as fast as she could to tend to the frightened horses.

Meanwhile, Debra and her husband slowly walked toward Courage, trying to understand what this anxious horse was trying to tell them. *Finally! COME ON!* Courage thought. He snaked his head and took off at a gallop toward Zander, who was barely hanging onto the man on the ground. Courage stopped and looked back to see if the humans were still following him. They followed but they were WAY too slow! "Come ON. We're running out of time!" he bucked and hollered. Courage decided to run to his friend and circle him hoping the humans would see the pair struggling on the ground. He stopped and reared for effect and watched them slowly and cautiously come. "Come on, come on, COME ON!" the frustrated stallion beckoned as he bucked and reared and blew out his nostrils as loud as he could. Then finally, all at once, it **HAPPENED!**

Chapter Sixteen

Lowell pulled up in his truck and saw Hillary holding two horses. He slowly followed her gaze and saw Zander's stallion with all four feet in the air carrying out the most amazing gymnastics he had ever seen out of a horse! Lowell drove slowly toward the stallion and saw a crowd inching their way toward the commotion. "What in the world is going on?" Lowell asked himself aloud. He saw what he thought to be two men on the ground struggling, and it appeared that one was Zander barely hanging onto the other man. He quickly pulled out his cell phone to call Zander's father and accelerated his truck as fast as he could go without startling the young stallion. "Mark! Get over to Phil and Debra's quick!" Lowell shouted into his cell phone and hung up as he jumped out of the vehicle and took off at a run.

At the same time, Debra and Phil finally figured out what the stallion was pointing them toward, so they took off at a run to help the boy, and the crowd quickly followed!

WHEW, it is about time! Courage thought. He immediately felt some of his tension melt away knowing help was finally coming. The concerned stallion turned toward his friend and watched the evil man hit his friend so hard that Zander yelled, "Please HELP!" Courage watched as the bad human started crawling away from Zander's grip, and Courage wasn't about to let that happen! "Oh, NO you DON'T!" the protective young stallion exclaimed. Courage trotted over to the man who was escaping from Zander's loosened grip. He stopped momentarily and then without any further thought the strong minded stallion stepped both front feet over the man, dropped to his knees and then collapsed over the man's legs, securing the bad man beneath his belly.

The young stallion finally relaxed knowing there was nothing the man would be able to do to hurt him or his friends so he calmly waited until everyone finally arrived.

Chapter Seventeen

Lowell ran to the scene and was astounded at what he just witnessed. He couldn't keep his eyes off this young stallion perched so confidently and peacefully over the man. He ran past Courage and kneeled next to Zander who was curled up in a ball and beat up pretty badly. "Son, are you okay?" Lowell asked Zander.

"I will be, thank you. Sir, did he....that man, get away?" Zander asked Lowell.

Lowell shifted his gaze back to Courage who was yawning as he silently rested on top of the man's legs. Lowell grinned, shook his head and replied to Zander, "No... No son, he is detained all right!" They heard the sirens coming toward them as the crowd from the barn quickly approached.

Mark and Rachel frantically pulled into the long driveway just ahead of the police cars. "Mark, look there's Shalot!" Rachel exclaimed with joy.

Mark pulled off the driveway to allow room for the squad cars to get by and suddenly saw the crowd approaching Courage who was lying down. "Rachel, I can't make out what is going on over there, but I think we better get over to Courage!" Mark said anxiously as he quickly jumped out of the truck. The couple ran to the young stallion as fast as they could, and as they came upon him, they could not believe their eyes, they were stunned beyond words to find Courage detaining Shalot's captor!

Meanwhile, Lowell helped Zander sit up and Mark and Rachel ran to their son's side. Zander finally got a look at Courage pinning

Shalot's abductor to the ground and he immediately burst out laughing. He laughed and laughed and laughed. He laughed so hard that Lowell and his parents started chuckling and then the crowd surrounding them joined in their laughter. It was the most amazing and funniest sight they had ever seen. Young Courage was a little startled by all the amusement, but he felt the mood lift and the energy lighten. Courage shook his head and mane, blew out his nostrils and pushed himself up off of the ground but continued to stand over the bad man. *JUST IN CASE!* Courage thought.

The man did not move a muscle. In fact, he didn't know if he could if he wanted to.

The police handcuffed the man and put him in the back of the squad car. Debra explained to the officers that she believed that this man had abandoned the little starved filly, Shalot, several days ago. The fireman suspected an intentionally set fire and Debra told the officers that she believed that this man could be the culprit because of past business disputes between him and her husband, Phil.

Mark, Rachel and Zander identified the man to the officers as Shalot's abductor and as the same man who tried to capture more horses on their neighbor's land. The officers informed the crowd that the man was wanted for other horse thefts and mistreatment of animals. The officers assured them that justice would be served. Everyone watched as the man, known as Ted Janks, was hauled away to jail in the back of the squad car. As they pulled out the long driveway the crowd cheered.

The raging fire was finally extinguished and it was starting to get dark and cold. Zander walked over to the young brave stallion who was eating grass with his eyes locked on the squad car pulling away. Zander scratched on the brave stallion's shoulder. "Courage..." he said and paused, "You are the most caring, determined and brave partner a human could ever ask for. Thank you so much for coming back to our family to accomplish our mission. We not only have our little filly back but we can be assured that Mr. Janks will never hurt another animal again." Zander swallowed hard and then asked the young stallion, "I'd love your home to be with me, that is if you want it to be?" He paused as a tear welled up in his eye then whispered. "You have more heart and desire than any being I know, horse or human and I love you." Courage didn't know the words the boy spoke but he felt his loving energy and that is all he needed to understand.

Chapter Eighteen

Everyone agreed including Hillary that Shalot would go home with Zander and Courage. Hillary wanted nothing more than the little filly to stay with her grandmother, but she knew the best thing for Shalot was to be with her own family and get healthy again.

That evening Zander and Courage walked proudly into their barn with big smiles on their faces. Mia looked up from eating her hay wondering where in the world they had been all day and then she saw Shalot. She couldn't believe her eyes – walking behind Zander was her daughter! "Shalot!" Mia whinnied with joy, "Oh Shalot, You are HOME! Thank you, Thank you, Thank you boys!" Mia excitedly proclaimed as she ran in circles inside her stall. She nickered to her daughter with so much love and happiness.

Shalot missed her mom so very much and all she wanted to do was be next to her. Shalot was so excited that she nickered back to her mother and started prancing. Zander opened Mia's stall and Shalot immediately rushed in. They nickered and chewed on each

other's withers, and they greeted each other with such love. Both Courage and Zander had tears in their eyes as they watched mother and daughter reunite.

Once the initial excitement wore down, Mia turned to Courage and spoke tenderly, "You will always have a place in our hearts young Courage. I hope you stay here forever! You are not only a brave stallion, YOU ARE AN AMAZING friend and we love you!" Mia nickered at Courage and turned her attention back to Shalot, "Baby girl, you need to put some weight on… Now EAT!" she ordered her daughter. The horses dove into their hay and settled in for the evening.

Chapter Nineteen

Over the next few days all was quiet on the Raven farm while Zander and Shalot recovered. Shalot ate lots of hay, and Mia was happy as could be watching over her little filly in the pasture. Courage had free reign of the property as he watched over his little herd and waited for his human friend to feel better.

During those long days, Courage waited for Zander to come outside and play with him. Every time the door to the boy's home opened he lifted his head from grazing to see if it was his friend. *Oh how he missed playing with him!* Young Courage thought to himself. Then finally on the third day, the door swung wide open and Zander walked out. Courage watched his friend slowly start to approach him, the boy stopped, made a kissing sound, and the excited stallion exuberantly trotted right to him. *Oh, I hope he scratches my itchy spots!* He thought as he dropped his head down, reaching his neck past his friend's hand hoping he would scratch just the right spot and HE DID! Zander spent quite a few minutes scratching Courage in all the places that the itchy stallion pointed out to him. Courage was in heaven! Oh how he loved his friend!

Zander felt a lot better today and thought he and Courage would make their way over to Lowell's to play with the filly. Zander placed the bareback pad on the confident stallion, and they headed out on the same path they took just a few days earlier to Lowell's training farm. Courage was more self-assured and happy to have a job as they trotted the path harmoniously. When they arrived at the facility, Zander put Courage in the paddock next to the miniature mule while he searched out Lowell. "Have fun you two!" Zander teased. The two munched on their hay eyeing one another as Zander walked away with a smile.

Zander meandered around the facility and met a few of Lowell's hands. They explained that Lowell was in a meeting and wouldn't be back for at least an hour but he was welcome to stick around and get familiar with the place.

Zander knew horses, he could thank his grandfather for that, but he didn't know much about horse racing, so he thought he would learn as much as possible while he had the opportunity. The boy watched the horses go for a gallop on the training track, and watched the trainers clock the horse's speed. It was amazing to Zander how fast some of these horses could run. The horses would finish their run, walk to cool down, get a bath, go back to their stalls or paddocks until the next day, then repeat this procedure all over again. Zander waited quite awhile for Lowell. Since things were starting to slow down on the track he thought he would ask if it was okay to take Courage for a spin.

Courage had been watching the horses run and wanted to run too. "I love to go FAST!" he told Korin, the miniature mule.

She smiled at young Courage. "Well, you'd fit in pretty well around here then!" she replied with a wink. "By the way, Cour…age…. I heard all about how you saved the day a few days ago, AND… they say it's not the first time," she said with a grin.

"Well, Miss Korin, the boy and I accomplished our mission and I am very grateful for that." he replied as he reached for more hay.

"Hmm – modest too. Well, anyway, I sure am sorry for giving you such a hard time. I must say I was impressed at how well you did today walking through the lane, no blankets chased you or anything!" she said with a laugh.

This time Courage knew that Korin was joking good-naturedly, and he just grinned.

Chapter Twenty

Zander approached the pen where he left Courage, and he saw that the mini mule and the relaxed stallion had made peace. "Well my friend, how about we go for a run?" Zander asked Courage with a big smile on his face.

Courage got so excited. "I'm going for a run! Woo Hoo!!" he exclaimed. He started trotting to Zander and then stopped cold. "Umm... I just understood what the boy said. How is that possible?" he turned and asked Korin in disbelief.

"Well – I don't know how to explain it – but it just happens. Something shifts inside of us when we choose to believe in ourselves and it becomes REALLY powerful when BOTH horse and human believe in EACH other!" Korin replied thoughtfully.

Courage stood yawning and shaking his head. "WOW! Wow, Wow, WOW!" He said to Korin with a yawn.

Korin laughed. "Hey, don't leave without coming over here and saying good-bye!" she urged with a grin.

He walked slowly back over to her, shaking his head and mane along the way, still in amazement of what just transpired with his human friend. Korin reached her head through the fence very carefully as Courage lowered his head to touch her nose. As they slowly touched, Korin quickly nipped him on the nose. "Ha, Gotcha!" she laughed.

He jumped back and trotted over to the boy, looking back at the mule.

"Hmph!" the surprised stallion uttered.

"See you around, young Courage!" Korin called to him with a smile.

"Yeah, see you around," Courage responded, displeased.

Zander grinned at the exchange between the mule and the stallion as he opened the gate for Courage to follow. The boy carried a borrowed exercise saddle in his arm and thought this would be a great transition from the bareback pad to a western saddle. He placed and cinched the lightweight saddle on Courage's back and moved him around. Courage accepted the exercise saddle just like he did the bareback pad – as if he had worn it for months.

Zander rode Courage out onto the track and noticed the stallion becoming more and more concerned about the other horses coming toward him at speed, so Zander spent some time getting the worried stallion's focus back on him.

At a walk Zander would ask the worried stallion to move his ribs over causing him to arc in a circle and once Zander felt young Courage relax, Zander would reward the calm stallion by moving forward again. They repeated this exercise instantly when Zander felt the young stallion start to get tense. The pair did this for almost one full lap around the one-mile training track until Courage started blowing out his nostrils and shaking his mane.

Zander smiled and asked young Courage into a trot. The pair jogged several laps around the track until Zander finally could feel Courage relax and maintain a nice rhythm. In that moment the boy knew the horse was ready to pick up the pace.

Zander asked Courage into a canter and then a gallop and just let him go, and they went *FAST!!!*

"Woo Hoo!" Courage hollered as he ran and ran and ran. "What fun!" Courage exclaimed. After they traveled at a run down the straightaway and through the turn, Zander slowed Courage back to a canter and then to a walk to cool the exhilarated stallion down. Both boys were overjoyed – they both loved the speed!

They walked off the track. Zander jumped off of Courage, rubbed him and started heading to the wash racks to give him a bath when he noticed Lowell and his trainer approaching them. Lowell shook Zander's hand with a grin, "Well son, this boy has plenty of heart and desire that's FOR SURE, we clocked Courage at :35 seconds in 3/8's of a mile. Only our REALLY good horses run at that speed. This boy really has something!" Lowell said with a smile.

"Do you know how he's bred?" the trainer asked Zander.

"Sir, he was in the wild, I have no idea!" Zander answered in surprise.

"You may want to think about getting him fit for racing. Let him run a race or two and see how he does." Lowell suggested.

"We will certainly consider it." Zander replied, astounded that they were THAT fast.

After Courage's bath, Zander got a tour of the facility. He met the filly he would start, and then the boys headed home. "Well Courage, not only are you a brave stallion, you are a fast stallion!" the boy expressed to Courage as he stroked his mane.

Courage was thrilled. He couldn't wait to tell his family. *I am big, brave and FAST!* He thought to himself. He puffed out his chest singing and prancing on the way home. "Woo, Hoo – I am a big, brave, FAST stallion. Oh Yes I am! I am FAST – I am FAST – I love to go FAST!" Zander laughed as Courage pranced along the trail on their way home.

When they arrived home, Zander gave Courage another bath and left him to graze. The boy's back was starting to ache, so he decided to call it a day. He went inside the house and shared the details of his day with his parents. He explained how fast Courage ran and Lowell's suggestion for Courage to train and race. His parents were supportive of whatever their son and young Courage wanted to do. They were proud of them both and were in awe of this talented horse that had blessed their family so many times over.

After awhile, Courage went behind the barn to graze by the mares' paddock, and as he looked up beyond the hill to watch the sunset, there stood Courage's father looking down at him. Courage focused hard on him and thought to himself, *Boy, oh boy, am I ever in trouble!*

Chapter Twenty-one

Courage slowly walked up the hill with his full attention on his father. The worried young stallion tried to read his father's expression as he approached him, but couldn't tell if his father was angry or pleased to see him. The closer he got to his father the more excited he became to tell him all about his visit with his friends. When he arrived at the top of the hill, Courage greeted his father and couldn't contain himself. The eager young stallion immediately blurted out the story of their mission. Courage explained how they had found Shalot and captured her abductor. He described how he got to run on a long dirt path that the human's called a track and how much fun it was to go fast. "And Father – the humans said that I run VERY FAST! They said I should be a race, um – a racehorse I think that is what they said. They thought it was in my blood, father. I really, REALLY like going fast!" Courage proudly exclaimed to his father with a gleam in his eye. He wanted to shout, "Father, I am not only a Big, Bad stallion... I am a FAST stallion!" but he thought better of it under the circumstances.

His father listened to everything that young Courage had to say and didn't respond for a few moments thinking about the best way to handle the situation. "Son, remember when I told you that your mother and I used to live amongst humans?" He asked.

"Yes sir." Courage responded.

"Well, there is a reason why you, my son, ARE fast, and I guess it's time I explain it all to you." his father spoke thoughtfully.

His father began telling young Courage about his family history and several minutes later, Mia and Shalot heard Courage explode in excitement. When they looked up on the hill, they could see the overjoyed stallion prancing, bucking, rearing and hollering, "Woo Hoo! I am A BIG, BRAVE, FAST Stallion! Oh yes I am, I am Fast... I AM FAST. OH YES I AM!" Courage shouted playfully. Mia and Shalot grinned at the young thrilled stallion up on the hill and his father... well his father just rolled his eyes and shook his head.

THE END .... or is it?

ABOUT THE AUTHOR

Theresa Fincher is passionate about horses and finds enjoyment in developing them. She has a passion for the Western Performance discipline. Her husband, Rhett, has a passion for horse racing and is employed in that field. They enjoy a lifestyle where horses are their main focus. Theresa studied several years with renowned horsemen Pat Parelli, Founder of Parelli Natural Horsemanship. She has a close working relationship with renowned horseman Martin Black and his wife Jennifer.

Theresa is the author of The Adventure of Courage, The Big, Bad Stallion Series: Prey meets Predator. She began writing this series in 2006 because of her love for the real connection to "the horse". She couldn't get enough of the communication and interaction with her horses, and she wanted to integrate that aspect into books for children who are also very passionate and in love with HORSES!

Theresa currently resides in Flower Mound TX, with her husband Rhett and three horses: Wriggley, Rabano, and Blue Smoke. Theresa founded ZennerYoga LLC, Fluidity Connection

Yoga DVD's and products and currently oversee's the ZennerYoga operation. Theresa has one daughter, Tianna Nelson, who resides in Minnesota with her husband Micah and their two children: Adrianna and Lowell James. You can go to:

The Adventures of Courage, Children's Book Series website:
www.couragethebigbadstallion.com

The Adventure of Courage's Facebook fanpage:
http://www.facebook.com/TheAdventuresOfCourageBookSeries?ref=hl

ZennerYoga's Facebook fanpage:
http://www.facebook.com/ZennerYoga?ref=hl

Fluidity Connection Website: http://www.fluidridingthruyoga.com/